Pickle Pizza

Beverly Lewis

Beverly Lewis Books for Young Readers

PICTURE BOOKS

Annika's Secret Wish
Cows in the House
Just Like Mama

THE CUL-DE-SAC KIDS

The Double Dabble Surprise
The Chicken Pox Panic
The Crazy Christmas Angel Mystery
No Grown-ups Allowed
Frog Power
The Mystery of Case D. Luc
The Stinky Sneakers Mystery
Pickle Pizza
Mailbox Mania
The Mudhole Mystery
Fiddlesticks
The Crabby Cat Caper
Tarantula Toes
Green Gravy
Backyard Bandit Mystery
Tree House Trouble
The Creepy Sleep-Over
The Great TV Turn-Off
Piggy Party
The Granny Game
Mystery Mutt
Big Bad Beans
The Upside-Down Day
The Midnight Mystery

Katie and Jake and the Haircut Mistake

www.BeverlyLewis.com

THE CUL-DE-SAC KIDS

Pickle Pizza

Beverly Lewis

BETHANY HOUSE PUBLISHERS
MINNEAPOLIS, MINNESOTA 55438

Published by Bethany House Publishers
11400 Hampshire Avenue South
Bloomington, Minnesota 55438
www.bethanyhouse.com

Bethany House Publishers is a Division of
Baker Book House Company, Grand Rapids, Michigan.

Printed in the United States of America

Library of Congress Cataloging-in-Publication Data

Lewis, Beverly
    Pickle pizza / by Beverly Lewis.
        p.   cm. — (Cul-de-sac kids ; 8)
    Summary: Hoping to surprise his grandfather on
Father's Day, Eric tries both a bird sculpture and a pickle
pizza and worries about the acceptability of both gifts.

    [1. Father's Day—Fiction. 2. Grandfathers—Fiction.
3. Artists—Fiction. 4. Pizza—Fiction.] I. Title.
II. Series: Lewis, Beverly, 1949–   Cul-de-sac kids ; 8.
PZ7.L58464Pi   1996
[Fic]—dc20   96–4440
ISBN 1–55661–728–3 (pbk.)   CIP
                                            AC

For
Matt Whiteis,
my pickle-lovin' fan.

THE CUL-DE-SAC KIDS

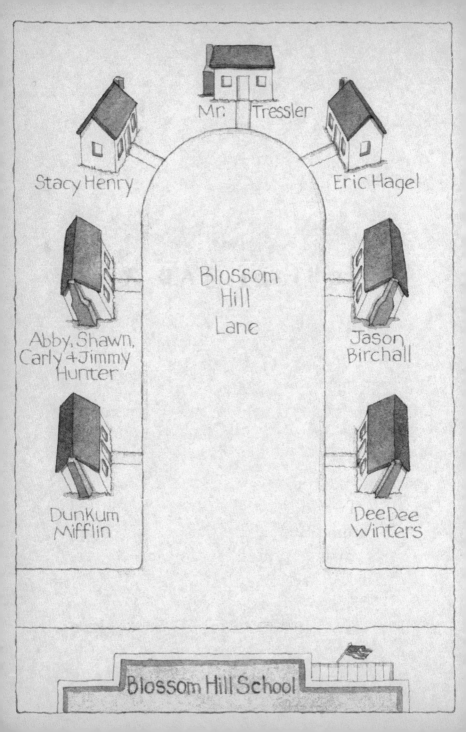

Mr. Tressler

Stacy Henry

Eric Hagel

Blossom Hill Lane

Abby, Shawn, Carly & Jimmy Hunter

Jason Birchall

Dunkum Mifflin

DeeDee Winters

Blossom Hill School

ONE

Eric Hagel was flat broke.

He sat in the dugout with his buddy Dunkum Mifflin. Eric shoved his bat into the dirt. "Only two days till Father's Day," he said.

"Two days—and I can't wait." Dunkum thumped his fist into his catcher's mitt. "My dad's gonna be so surprised."

Eric was silent.

Dunkum kept talking. "I bought a

giant crossword-puzzle book. My dad has a puzzle habit, you know."

Eric nodded. "Did you buy it with your own money?"

"I saved up for a couple weeks," Dunkum said.

Eric wished he had money of his own. He wanted to buy a Father's Day present for his grandpa who lived with them.

There wasn't much money to go around. His mom baked special-order cakes for extra money. Grandpa repaired watches, but his eyes weren't strong anymore. He worked only three afternoons a week.

"What about you?" Dunkum asked. "Have you been saving up?"

"Not much. My paper route money goes to the family," Eric answered. He'd had the route for a whole year. But there never seemed to be money left over. At least not enough for a Father's Day present.

"Are you going to celebrate with your grandpa?" Dunkum asked.

Eric smiled. "He's been kinda like a father to me since my dad died. Only one thing . . ."

"What's that?" Dunkum asked.

"I'm broke. I can't buy anything."

Dunkum stood up. "Why don't you make something?"

Jason Birchall walked up to them. "Make what? What are we talking about?"

Eric shrugged his shoulders. "It's about Father's Day. Dunkum thinks I should make something for Grandpa."

"Sure, why not?" Jason said. "Some of the other Cul-de-sac Kids are making things."

Dunkum nodded. "Abby Hunter always says, 'homemade gifts are the best.' "

Eric got up and swung his bat around. "Sounds good. But *what*? What can I make?"

Eric, Dunkum, and Jason made a huddle. A think-huddle.

"What does your grandpa like?" Dunkum asked.

Eric thought a moment. "Birds. He's bird-crazy."

Jason started laughing.

Eric frowned. "What's so funny?"

"I saw him spying on a bird's nest yesterday," Jason replied. "He was up on his step stool—wearing those weird field glasses."

"They're *not* weird," Eric said. "They come in handy sometimes." He was thinking about last Christmas. Grandpa's field glasses had helped solve a mystery. "Remember those crazy Christmas angels next door?" Eric asked. "At Mr. Tressler's house?"

"Hey, you're right!" Jason said, laughing. "Remember those Christmas cookies Dee Dee and Carly made?"

Dunkum's eyes lit up. "And Stacy made a card with gold glitter. Remember that?"

"Hey! I have an idea," Jason said. "Why don't you ask Stacy about her art class?"

Eric's mouth pinched up. "Why should I?"

"Because Stacy's a good artist," Dunkum stated. "Maybe she'll give you some ideas for Father's Day."

"Or maybe she'll take you to art class with her," Jason said. He danced around like it was a big deal.

Eric shook his head. "How can I get her to invite me?"

Jason laughed. "Just ask her, silly. She doesn't bite."

Eric's face got red. "I know that."

"Then ask her," Jason teased.

Eric scratched his head. "I'll think about it."

TWO

Eric ate supper fast.

It was still light out when he finished. He dashed across the street to Stacy Henry's house.

She opened the door. "Hi," Stacy said.

"Hi," Eric said back. He didn't know what else to say.

"What do you want?" she asked.

"Oh . . . uh, nothing." Then he remembered what Dunkum said. "I heard

17

you were making something."

Stacy's face burst into a grin. "I'm working on a gift for my dad—for Father's Day."

"Oh." The rest of the words got stuck in Eric's throat. The words he couldn't speak.

"My dad's coming on Sunday," she said. "I haven't seen him since Easter."

Eric remembered. The Cul-de-sac Kids had surprised their parents with an Easter pet parade. Stacy's dad had come to see it, too.

"I'm glad about your dad," Eric said.

She nodded. "I can't wait. I really miss him."

Eric understood. He missed his dad, too.

"What are you making?" Eric asked.

Stacy opened the door. "Come in. I'll show you."

Eric followed Stacy downstairs. They

went through the family room and into a smaller room.

"This is my new art room," Stacy said. "My mom and I just finished it."

Eric looked around.

An easel stood at one end of the room with paints and brushes. There were drawings hanging on the wall. "Wow," Eric said. "This is really great."

"It used to be a storage room," Stacy explained. "My mom decided I should have a place to work."

Eric spotted a lump of green clay on the worktable. "What's that?" he asked.

"Just some practice clay. But look what else I'm sculpting." She opened a cabinet door. Stacy reached in and pulled out an eagle sculpture. She held it high. "What do you think?"

"It's terrific!" Eric couldn't believe his eyes.

Stacy smiled. "I hope Daddy likes it."

"I'm sure he will," Eric said.

Stacy smiled and set the eagle down.

Eric crept over to Stacy's worktable. He studied the eagle. The wings were folded down, close to the bird's body. The eagle's head was turned toward one wing. "What's it made of?" Eric asked.

"Sculpey."

"What's that?" Eric asked.

"It's like soft clay. You bake it in the oven, and it gets hard. When it cools off, you can paint it."

"Wow," Eric whispered. He wished he could make something like this. For Grandpa.

"Here, feel it," Stacy said.

Eric reached out with his pointer finger. Gently, he touched the eagle's head. "It feels smooth. No bumps or lumps."

Stacy nodded. "Thanks. I worked hard."

Eric stood up. He looked at Stacy. *Should I ask about going to her art class?* he wondered.

"What are you staring at?" Stacy asked.

Eric looked away. "I . . . uh . . . oh, nothing."

Father's Day was coming fast. Would Stacy invite him to art class?

Eric hoped so. He *really* hoped so.

THREE

Eric couldn't stop thinking about the art class.

"I wonder if—" He stopped.

Stacy blinked her eyes. "What did you say?"

Eric tried again. "I . . . er . . . AUURGH!" The words didn't want to come out. Not the ones he wanted to say.

Stacy's eyes grew wide.

At last, Eric said, "I like your eagle sculpture. Thanks for showing me."

Stacy grinned. "Anytime."

"Well, see ya," Eric said.

Stacy walked upstairs with him. "Thanks for coming," she said.

"Goodbye." The screen door slapped shut behind him.

Eric clumped down the sidewalk. He wished he'd asked about the art class. He wished he weren't so shy sometimes.

Zippo! A flash of green leaped past him.

Something green with skinny legs.

Jason's frog, Croaker, was loose!

Eric chased after the bullfrog. "Come back!" he called.

Croaker
 hopped
  all
   the
    way
     down
      Blossom Hill Lane.

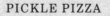

Eric ran after the frog. "Croaker, come back!"

Boink! The frog leaped into a bush in front of Dunkum's house. Out of sight.

Eric got down on his knees. He pushed the branches back. But Croaker was out of reach.

"What're you doing in there, Croaker?" Eric called.

Suddenly he heard footsteps. Eric turned around.

It was Jason Birchall.

"Who are you talking to?" Jason asked.

"To your frog." Eric pointed to the bush. "He disappeared in there."

Jason leaned down and peered into the bush.

"How'd he get loose?" Eric asked.

"Your grandpa came over to borrow some sugar. He wanted to see my frog up close," Jason explained. "So I took

Croaker out of the aquarium."

Eric scratched his head. "My grandpa wanted to see your frog?"

"Yep." Jason stood up and brushed off his jeans. "And he said something really weird."

"Like what?" Eric asked.

"Something like: frogs and pickles look alike." Jason laughed.

"Hey, don't make fun."

Jason poked playfully at Eric. "Frogs and pickles *do* have something in common."

"Yeah. They're both green," Eric said. "And they have bumps."

Jason pushed up his glasses. "How do frogs taste?"

Eric laughed out loud. "That's gross! But some *pickles* are sweet. My favorite!"

"Not me," Jason said. "I like *dill* pickles."

"So does my grandpa." Eric thought

about Father's Day again. "Are you making something for your dad?"

"First I have to find my frog." Jason inched around the bush, looking.

"Well, good luck finding your four-legged pickle," Eric teased.

Frogs and pickles. Grandpa should do stand-up comedy!

Quickly, Eric headed up the cul-de-sac. He wanted to stop by Stacy's house again.

He stuck out his chin. *This* time he'd get brave. He would invite himself to Stacy's art class.

It was now or never!

FOUR

Eric ran up the steps to Stacy's house.

He could see inside the screen door. Sunday Funnies wagged his fluffy tail.

"Hey there, boy," Eric said.

The white cockapoo always found the Sunday comics first. That's why he had such a silly name.

Sunday Funnies yipped and jumped up.

Eric hoped Stacy would hear her

puppy. He wanted her to come to the door, so he wouldn't have to knock.

Seconds passed, but Stacy didn't come.

Eric decided to knock. A soft, shy knock. The screen door flapped gently against the frame.

He waited.

Sunday Funnies kept barking and running around. He wanted to play.

At last, Stacy came to the door.

Eric stood tall. "Hi, again."

"Hi." She stared at him.

Eric felt silly. He looked down at his sneakers.

"What's wrong?" Stacy asked.

"Uh . . . nothing."

"Really?" she said.

"It's just . . ." He was having trouble saying it.

"Why don't you say what you're

thinking?" Stacy opened the screen door and came outside.

OK, here goes, Eric thought. He took a deep breath. "Can I go to your art class tomorrow?"

"*Can* you?" There was a twinkle in her eye. "I don't know if you can."

"I can't?" Eric asked.

Stacy frowned. "Are you allowed to come?"

"Allowed?" Eric was mixed up.

"Yeah, did you ask your mom?"

Eric shook his head. "Not yet."

"Well, the correct way to ask is: '*May* I go with you?' "

Eric sat on the front step.

"Just remember, *can* means able to," Stacy said. "*May* means allowed to."

Eric sighed. He hadn't expected a speech lesson.

"OK," Stacy said, smiling. "That's settled." She pulled a piece of green bubble gum out of her pocket. "Want some?"

"Sure, thanks." Eric stuffed the gum in his mouth.

Stacy opened a piece of pink bubble gum for herself.

"I want to make a bird tomorrow," Eric said. "What's the name of that stuff again?"

"Sculpey."

Eric smiled. "That's what I'm going to use."

"Good choice," she said.

Whamo! Eric socked the air.

Now he felt good.

Just then, Eric spotted Jason across the street. He had Croaker between both hands. And he was running.

"Hey, Jason!" Eric called to him.

Jason glanced over his shoulder. "I finally caught my frog. It took all this time." Then he hurried into his house.

Eric blew a giant green bubble. He thought about Grandpa wanting to see Croaker up close. And he thought about Father's Day.

His sculpting project was going to be perfect. Eric couldn't wait to get started.

I'll have to work hard, he thought. *Father's Day is almost here!*

FIVE

It was Saturday. At last!

Eric delivered newspapers extra early. Extra fast.

When he was finished, he came home and took a shower. Then he dressed for art class.

Eric tiptoed into Grandpa's room.

Z-z-ziz-zaz-zuk! The snoring shook the old bed.

Eric crept past the dresser. Past the closet. He peeked into Grandpa's book-case.

Good! The bird book was there. Eric slid it under his arm. He would borrow it for the class.

★　★　★

Stacy was waiting outside when Eric arrived. She was holding a small box. Her unpainted eagle was inside.

Eric showed her the big book. The bird book.

"Wow," she said. "This is great."

They sat on the step looking at the book. Stacy turned the pages carefully. "What bright colors! And the pictures are so big."

"Grandpa likes them that way."

Stacy said softly, "I hope his eyes get better."

"Me too," Eric said. "Grandpa wears a magnifying glass when he repairs watches. But not when he's looking at this book."

Stacy smiled. "He wears his field glasses for bird watching, too."

Eric smiled back. "Watching birds is his favorite thing. But his eyes are getting weak."

"Then your idea is perfect," she said. "Sculptures are great to touch. Even if your grandpa loses his sight, he'll be able to *feel* your bird!"

Eric hadn't thought of that.

Soon it was time to leave for art class. Stacy's mom was a careful driver. But Eric wished she would zoom around the corners. To make the time pass, he studied the bird book.

At last, they arrived in front of a red-brick house. A white sign hung from the lamppost. It said: *Young Artists' Studio.*

Stacy's mom waved goodbye and pulled away from the curb. Eric followed Stacy up the stony walkway.

"This is where I come every Saturday," she said. They went inside. Rows of sketches, cartoons, and paintings decorated the walls. A dark-haired lady sat behind a wide desk.

Stacy went up to the desk. "This is my friend Eric," she told the lady. "He's my guest today."

"Welcome." The desk lady smiled.

Stacy turned to Eric. "Eric, this is Miss Lana. She signs kids up for classes."

Eric grinned. "I'd like to sign up sometime."

"We'd love to have you," Miss Lana said.

Stacy and Eric headed down the hall. In the sculpting studio, Eric counted ten kids at work.

"Follow me," Stacy said. Her table was small and flat like all the others. A set of paints and some brushes were there.

Mr. Albert came over. "Nice to see you, Stacy," her teacher said.

Stacy introduced Eric. "Eric's one of the Cul-de-sac Kids. It's a club." She explained about the seven houses on their block. "We have nine kids on Blossom Hill Lane. Most of us are making something for Father's Day."

Eric listened.

Stacy continued. "Eric wants to make a bird out of sculpey." She didn't say it was for his grandpa. Maybe she didn't want to say that Eric's dad had died.

Eric looked at her. *Stacy's a good friend*, he thought.

The teacher scooted a table next to Stacy's. He found an extra chair. "There we are," said Mr. Albert. "I will be glad to help you, Eric."

"Thanks." Eric showed him the bird book and the picture of a red robin. The teacher gave him some basic pointers.

Then he went to help another student.

Stacy got Eric started. She stuck her hands into his sculpey. Right into the middle of it. She worked it like bread dough. "There, that's how to begin. Now *you* try."

Eric stared at the white clump. He picked it up. The sculpey felt cool in his hands. And a little hard.

Smasho!

He jammed it between his hands.

Stacy grinned. "That's it!"

Eric glanced at Stacy's eagle. What a beautiful sculpture—the smooth body and graceful wings.

He stared at his blob of nothing.

Flip-flop.

Eric's stomach lurched.

Beside him, Stacy began to paint. He watched her work. Then he looked down at his table. *Ee-e-yew*, he thought. *This*

glob is supposed to be a Father's Day present?

Eric pulled his fingers out of the sculpey. They were shaking. *What am I doing here?*

SIX

Eric's heart was pounding.

He got up and left the room. He stood in the hallway.

Stacy rushed out. "What's wrong, Eric?"

He stared at the floor. "I don't belong here."

Stacy grabbed his arm. "You'll never know if you don't try."

Eric knew she was right. "What if it turns out all yucky?" he asked.

Stacy said, "Just do your best. That's what counts."

Eric agreed to try.

He went back into the classroom with Stacy. He walked past young artists. He saw their small statues. Dolphins, lions, a clown, and even a T-rex. This was work in progress.

Eric sat at his table and took a deep breath. He picked up the bird book and flipped through the pages. The red robin picture was on page 33.

With his finger, he traced the lines of its round shape. He was ready to form the body. Next came the tiny head, and wings.

Eric worked for two hours. Several times, Mr. Albert came to help and give advice. Stacy helped, too.

By the end of class, Eric's work in progress was only half finished. He frowned. "Tomorrow's Father's Day. I can't give this mess to my grandpa."

Stacy said, "Just tell him you're working on a top-secret project. When the sculpture's done, give it to him."

Eric shook his head. "It might take weeks. I want something for *tomorrow*!"

"What's wrong with giving him the unfinished robin?" she asked.

"I just told you." Eric put his robin glob in a box. "It isn't done."

Stacy wiggled her nose. Off she went to clean up her work area.

Mr. Albert stopped by. Eric thanked him for his help.

"Perhaps you can join us," Mr. Albert suggested.

"I'd like that," Eric said. But he knew it was impossible. Besides, he wasn't an artist.

Eric went outside to wait for Stacy. He gripped his cardboard box. On top of it, he carried the bird book. Inside the box was a blobby globby robin.

One after another, the young artists came with their sculptures. Eric tried not to stare.

If only my sculpture were finished! he thought. *If only I could come to class like Stacy all the time.*

Father's Day tomorrow—and no present. Eric felt sorry for his grandpa.

He felt sorry for himself, too.

SEVEN

Honk! Honk!

Eric and Stacy ran to get in the car.

"How was art class?" Stacy's mother asked.

Stacy glanced at Eric. "I finished painting my eagle."

Eric slumped down in the backseat. The bird book lay on the seat beside him.

"What about you, Eric?" Stacy's mother asked.

"I . . . uh, it was nice." Eric thought

about the class. Mr. Albert and Miss Lana. Stacy and the other kids. All of them had been very nice.

The NOT nice thing was in his box. The yucko bird sculpture!

Eric put the box on the floor—and stuck his tongue out at it.

Stacy and her mom were talking in the front seat. They were making Father's Day plans. They were planning how to gift wrap the eagle sculpture.

Eric slapped his hands over his ears. He didn't want to hear about Father's Day. He didn't want to hear about Stacy's eagle.

A lump choked Eric's throat. He missed his dad.

But he had a terrific grandpa. Eric wanted him to know how special he was. Very special.

Sometimes at night, Eric would tiptoe down the hall. He'd peek into Grand-

pa's room and listen. In the darkness, he could hear Grandpa talking to God. "Please bless Eric, my grandson," Grandpa would say.

Those prayers made Eric feel good. And strong.

★ ★ ★

Stacy turned around in the front seat. Her eyes were kind.

Eric took his hands away from his ears.

"Are you OK?" Stacy asked.

Eric shrugged his shoulders.

Just then, Stacy's mom made a left turn. The box holding Eric's project slid toward the door. The unfinished bird rolled out. Eric kept his seat belt on. He stared at the bird.

When the car pulled into the driveway, Eric picked up his sculpture. Quickly, he scooped it into the box. He climbed out of the car. "Thanks for taking me."

"Remember what I told you," Stacy said. "You can finish your sculpture later. Then give it to your grandpa." Her voice was soft.

"I know," Eric said. But more than anything he wanted something for tomorrow. Tomorrow was the day Grandpa deserved a special gift.

Eric closed the lid on the box and headed for home. Someday he would finish the sculpture. Maybe for Grandpa's birthday. Or Christmas.

But *today* he would think of something. Something to give Grandpa for Father's Day.

There was no time to waste!

EIGHT

Eric carried the box upstairs. He shoved it under his bed. Then he went to Grandpa's room to return the bird book.

Eric decided to go outside.

Carly Hunter was making chalk drawings on the sidewalk. Big, bright drawings.

Dee Dee Winters, Carly's best friend, came skating down the sidewalk.

"Hello-o, Eric!" Dee Dee called.

Eric wandered over to the girls. He

stood there quietly with his hands in his pockets.

Carly looked up at him. "Aren't you talking?"

Eric shook his head. "Not much."

"How come?" Dee Dee asked.

"Long story," Eric said. He was thinking about Father's Day. Again.

Carly stood up. She put her arm around Dee Dee. "Well, maybe *we* can help."

Dee Dee agreed. "Yeah, we make a mean batch of cookies." She turned to Carly. "Baking cookies—and eating them—always helps if you're sad." Dee Dee's face burst into a big smile. "That's what we made for Father's Day gifts."

Whamo! An idea struck Eric.

His hands flew out of his pockets. "Got any recipe books?"

"Do I ever!" Dee Dee said.

"Can I borrow one?" Eric asked.

"You mean—*may* you?" Dee Dee said.

Eric smiled to himself. Another speech lesson?

"Wait here!" Dee Dee skated down the street.

When she came back, Dee Dee showed off her favorite recipes.

Carly peered at the book. Then at Eric. "Are *you* gonna bake cookies?"

Eric stared at the recipe book. He scratched his head. "Maybe."

Beep, beep! Dunkum and Jason came riding their bikes. "Look out!" yelled Jason.

Eric played along and acted scared. He jumped onto the sidewalk. Dunkum and Jason dropped their bikes on the grass.

"What's up?" asked Jason.

"Nothin' much," Eric said.

Dunkum spotted the recipe book.

"Are you making Father's Day cookies?" he asked Eric.

"I'm thinking about it," Eric said.

Dee Dee was still looking at her book. "Hey! Here's pizza recipes!"

"So?" Dunkum said.

"I *love* pizza!" Dee Dee said.

"Me too," Eric said. He went to look at the book.

Carly put down her colored chalk. "Let's see how many pizza recipes are in there." She squeezed between Dee Dee and Eric to have a look.

While Carly counted, Eric's brain whirled. *Homemade pizza for Father's Day*, he thought. *What a great idea!*

★ ★ ★

After lunch, Eric read the pizza recipe. It was called, "The Perfect Pizza."

Eric chuckled to himself. His pizza was going to be more than perfect. It was going to be a surprise.

The best Father's Day pizza ever!

NINE

Eric sat at the kitchen table. He opened Dee Dee's recipe book.

His mother dried her hands. "Looks like someone's going to cook," she said.

"I'm gonna try."

She leaned over his shoulder. "Mm-m, pizza. Good idea."

"Sh-h! It's a secret for Grandpa," Eric said. "For Father's Day."

"Need some help?" Mrs. Hagel's eyes twinkled. "I'm a pro, you know."

"You can help me," he said. "You can keep Grandpa out of the kitchen."

"It's a deal." She closed the kitchen door.

"Work in progress." Eric chuckled softly.

In the cupboard, he found the flour, salt, and pepper. In the fridge, he found the eggs and milk.

Suddenly he spotted the pickle jar.

Dill pickles!

Grandpa loved pickles. He ate pickles with everything. Scrambled eggs and pickles. Mashed potatoes and pickles. Broccoli, peas, and carrots—all with pickles. He even ate pickles with apple pie!

Eric grabbed the pickle jar. "My pizza *will* be perfect," he said out loud. "A perfect pickle pizza!"

Quickly, he set to work. He grated the cheese. Lots of it. Next, he made the

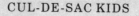

dough for the crust. After that, Eric opened a can of pizza sauce.

Then he chopped the pickles on the cutting board. *What a great topping*, he thought as he chopped.

Thirty minutes later, the pizza was ready for topping. Eric took it out of the oven. He sprinkled on extra cheese and pizza sauce. And piles of chopped pickles.

Then he slid the pan back into the oven. The timer was set. Ten minutes to go.

Soon the smell of hot dill filled the kitchen. He couldn't wait to taste his perfect pizza.

Buzz-zing! The timer went off.

Eric removed the pan from the oven. Carefully, he cut ten pieces.

Tap, tap. Someone knocked on the back door.

He hurried to open it.

There stood Carly and Dee Dee with

a plateful of cookies. "Hi, again," Carly said, giggling.

Eric gazed at the cookies.

"We're having a taste test," Dee Dee said. "Help yourself."

"Thanks!" Eric bit into a chocolate chip cookie. "Mm-m, it's great!"

"Goody!" said Carly.

Dee Dee sniffed the air. "Hey, what's that smell?"

"My Father's Day pizza," Eric said.

Carly wrinkled her nose. "It smells . . . uh, funny."

Then Eric had an idea. "Wait here," he said and raced back inside.

In a flash, he was back with his pickle pizza. "Who wants to taste *my* baking?" he asked.

Dee Dee crept up to the pizza. Her eyes got very big. "What's in it?"

"Just taste it," Eric insisted.

"Uh . . . I don't know," Carly said.

Carly and Dee Dee stared at the pizza.

"You go first," Dee Dee said to Carly.

"No, *you*," Carly said.

Eric stepped between them. He handed each girl a piece of pizza. "Here. Taste it together," he said. "On your mark, get set . . . bite!"

Carly and Dee Dee bit into Eric's pickle pizza. They coughed and spit it out.

Dee Dee began to gag. "This is gross!"

Eric's heart sank. *My pizza is a flop!*

He snatched up the pizza and ran into the house.

Back inside, Eric wrapped up the pizza slices. He shoved them way back in the fridge. Maybe he'd feed Grandpa's birds tomorrow. *If* he could get them to eat pickle pizza pieces!

Feeling sad, Eric went to his room.

He looked at the calendar beside his bed. Saturday, June 15. Father's Day was almost here. There was nothing to give Grandpa.

Time had run out.

TEN

The Hagels went to church the next day. Eric sat between his grandpa and mother.

After church, Eric helped set the dining room table. He went to the kitchen for some napkins. That's when he saw Grandpa poking around in the fridge.

"What's this?" Grandpa held up a slice of cold pizza.

"Nothing you'd want to eat," Eric said.

Grandpa unwrapped a slice. "Are you sure?"

"It's terrible. It's—" Eric stopped.

"What's wrong with it?"

Eric stared at the floor. "It was supposed to be your Father's Day present. But it turned out yucky. I'm real sorry."

Grandpa touched Eric's shoulder. "It's the thought that counts."

"Maybe the birds will eat it," Eric said.

Grandpa didn't answer. He took a dish out of the cupboard. But his eyes were on the pizza.

Then he put the pizza in the microwave to reheat.

What's he doing? Eric wondered.

He remembered yesterday's taste test. Dee Dee and Carly hated his pizza. They'd even spit it out!

The timer bell rang. The pizza was warm. Grandpa blew on it gently. Then

he bit into the pickle pizza.

Eric held his breath. Would Grandpa gag, too?

There was a long silence.

Then Grandpa's face lit up. "This is wonderful! Simply wonderful!"

Eric couldn't believe his ears. Or his eyes! "You like it?" he asked.

Grandpa's face wrinkled up in the biggest smile ever. "This is a *grand* Father's Day present!"

Eric hugged him. "Really?"

"You know I love pickles." Grandpa was grinning.

Eric's mother came into the kitchen. She was carrying the box from art class.

Eric rushed over to her. He whispered, "Where'd you find that?"

"Under your bed," she said. "I was looking for your shoes and there it was."

Eric's eyes darted to Grandpa. He pulled his mom out of the kitchen. "I don't want Grandpa to know about this yet," he explained. "It's a sculpting project."

She smiled. "I can see that. And I want you to finish it."

"Someday." Eric closed the lid.

"How about this summer?" she said. "Mr. Albert called yesterday."

"From the art studio?" Eric asked.

She nodded. "He wants to give you a grant for art lessons."

"He's going to *pay* for my art classes?"

"Are you interested?" she asked.

"Are pickles green?" Eric hugged his mother.

"That must be a yes," she said.

Grandpa peeked his head around the corner. "What's all the whispering?"

Eric's mother told the exciting news. She told Grandpa without saying a word about the robin in the box. The robin that was waiting to be finished.

"Well, what do you know! We have an artist in the house." Grandpa winked at Eric. "And a wonderful chef!"

Eric stood tall. And reached for a slice of pickle pizza.

THE CUL-DE-SAC KIDS SERIES
Don't miss #9!

MAILBOX MANIA

Abby Hunter has big plans for the Fourth of July. As president of the Cul-de-sac Kids, she declares "Mailbox Mania" on Blossom Hill Lane. The kids decorate their mailboxes. And choose a judge to vote for a winner.

As the holiday comes closer, the Cul-de-sac Kids argue. Carly and Dee Dee threaten to drop out of the club. Jason tries to outdo everyone. Soon all the kids are battling.

Then a mysterious present shows up in each of their mailboxes. Who hid the presents there? And why?

Also by Beverly Lewis

GIRLS ONLY (GO!)
Youth Fiction

Dreams on Ice   Follow the Dream
Only the Best   Better Than Best
A Perfect Match   Photo Perfect
Reach for the Stars   Star Status

SUMMERHILL SECRETS
Youth Fiction

Whispers Down the Lane   House of Secrets
Secret in the Willows   Echoes in the Wind
Catch a Falling Star   Hide Behind the Moon
Night of the Fireflies   Windows on the Hill
A Cry in the Dark   Shadows Beyond the Gate

HOLLY'S HEART
Youth Fiction

Best Friend, Worst Enemy   Straight-A Teacher
Secret Summer Dreams   No Guys Pact
Sealed With a Kiss   Little White Lies
The Trouble With Weddings   Freshman Frenzy
California Crazy   Mystery Letters
Second-Best Friend   Eight Is Enough
Good-Bye, Dressel Hills   It's a Girl Thing

ABRAM'S DAUGHTERS
Adult Fiction

The Covenant   The Betrayal

THE HERITAGE OF LANCASTER COUNTY
Adult Fiction

The Shunning   The Confession
The Reckoning

OTHER ADULT FICTION

The Postcard   •   The Crossroad

The Redemption of Sarah Cain

October Song

Sanctuary*   •   The Sunroom

www.BeverlyLewis.com

*with David Lewis

ABOUT THE AUTHOR

Beverly Lewis loves dill pickles. When she was little, she even drank pickle juice! Now she saves it to make potato salad for her pickle-lovin' husband and kids.

Beverly's idea for this story came from her twins, Jon and Janie, who are young artists. (You *can* learn to draw, sculpt, or paint. Remember: you never know till you try!)

Come laugh and solve mysteries with Beverly Lewis and the Cul-de-sac Kids in all the books of the series.

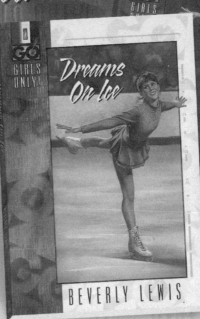

From Bethany House Publishers

Series for Beginning Readers*

Young Cousins Mysteries
by Elspeth Campbell Murphy
Rib-tickling mysteries just for beginning readers—with Timothy, Titus, and Sarah-Jane from the Three Cousins Detective Club®.

Watch Out for Joel!
by Sigmund Brouwer
Seven-year-old Joel is always getting into scrapes—despite his older brother, Ricky, always being told, "Watch out for Joel!"

Series for Young Readers†

AstroKids™
by Robert Elmer
Space scooters? Floating robots? Jupiter ice cream? Blast into the future for out-of-this-world, zero-gravity fun with the AstroKids on space station *CLEO-7*.

The Cul-de-sac Kids
by Beverly Lewis
Each story in this lighthearted series features the hilarious antics and predicaments of nine endearing boys and girls who live on Blossom Hill Lane.

Janette Oke's Animal Friends
by Janette Oke
Endearing creatures from the farm, forest, and zoo discover their place in God's world through various struggles, mishaps, and adventures.

Three Cousins Detective Club®
by Elspeth Campbell Murphy
Famous detective cousins Timothy, Titus, and Sarah-Jane learn compelling Scripture-based truths while finding—and solving—intriguing mysteries.

*(ages 6–8)   †(ages 7–10)